10 Stories to Make a Difference is a collection of ten original illustrated stories for young readers, all inspired by the theme of *difference*. The collection features a mix of well-known and emerging writers and illustrators, giving a platform to untold stories and diverse new voices. Produced by Pop Up Projects, a non-profit, UK-based national children's literature development agency, 10 Stories celebrates Pop Up's 10th birthday in 2021. Proceeds from sales supports Pop Up's work in deprived schools, marginalised communities, and with talented writers and illustrators, especially from backgrounds that are under-represented in children's publishing. 10 Stories will be an annual publishing event, with a whole new collection planned for 2022.

Find out more at **www.pop-up.org.uk**

Krista M. Lambert writes stories for young readers to further acceptance and love of the self and of others. Originally from Texas, USA, she is currently studying Creative Writing at Stephen F Austin University. When not writing she enjoys gardening, reading, and playing with her cat. Krista was one of four young winners of Pop Up's 10th Birthday Writing Competition in 2020; *Indigo Takes Flight* was chosen out of 100s of entries from 40 countries, and is Krista's first published children's book.

Chris Riddell is an illustrator, writer and political cartoonist for *The Observer*. His many books for children include the bestselling series' *Goth Girl* and *Ottoline*, as well as *Coraline, The Graveyard Book, The Sleeper and the Spindle* and *Pirate Stew* (all with Neil Gaiman). He was Waterstones Children's Laureate 2015-2017, won the prestigious CILIP Kate Greenaway Medal no less than three times, and was awarded an OBE for services to children's literature in 2019. He lives in Brighton with his family.

Edited & art directed by **Holly Tonks**, Lantana

Publisher **Dylan Calder**
Coordinator **Amanda Saakwa-Mante**
Designer **Txabi Jones**

INDIGO
TAKES FLIGHT

Written by
Krista M. Lambert

Illustrated by
Chris Riddell

Once upon a time,
far away, long ago,
there lived a little boy
who was called Indigo.

Indigo was funny,
Indigo was smart,
but this lad, he had a secret
tucked away against his heart.

He carried something heavy,
something awkward, something cold.
Inside his cape he hid it;
it was hard for him to hold.

Indigo did his very best
to throw his burden down.
Yet always it was waiting
when next he turned around.

He dreaded what might happen,
for he knew without a doubt
the world would not accept him,
if anyone found out.

He did not tell his father,
he could not tell his mum,
for he thought, "They'll surely hate me
when they know what I've become."

His mind grew dark and restless.
His face grew sad and shamed.
His friends asked what could hurt him,
but he left his pain unnamed.

What was our hero's secret,
so awful and forbidden?
Just this: beneath his cloak, you see,
a dragon's egg was hidden.

No other soul could spot it;
only Indigo could tell.
But bit by bit was growing
a crack upon the shell.

"Soon, all will know my secret.
Soon, everyone will see.
And when they have discovered,
the world will run from me."

Our boy, he tried to hide it:
he lied to all the land,
so scared he was of something that
he could not understand.

His efforts did not slow it.
The crack, it grew the more.
His load was weighing heavier
beneath the cloak he wore.

One day, he was not watching;
he'd quite forgot his egg.
But when he least expected,
something scaly brushed his leg . . .

A tiny baby dragon,
glowing green and blue and black,
wove in between his ankles
and prowled around his back.

His egg at last had opened;
his nightmare had come true.
This monster would not leave him—

What was our boy to do?

He gasped, but called to no one;
he could not let them see.
"Alone," he whispered through his tears,
"is what I'll have to be."

He left his friends, his family.
He set out to make a plan.
He turned from those he loved
as only fearful children can.

At first, he tried pretending
that his dragon was not real,
but the more that he denied it,
the more dragon he could feel.

The youth next thought, "I'll flee it!"
He ran swiftly through the dell,
but his beast grew only closer
the faster his feet fell.

"I hate you!" our boy told it.
"Leave me be! Go far away!"
But his dragon grew much stronger
with each curse he found to say.

He drew his sword to fight it;
he tried to kill it dead.
But when he struck his dragon down
it rose again, instead!

By then, the beast was frightful—
it had grown three times its size.
"My cape won't hide the creature now,"
he thought, "nor will my lies."

When strangers saw him coming,
they did what he most feared:
with one look at his dragon,
they turned and disappeared.

His dragon scared the neighbours.
It frightened dogs and sheep.
It passed a laughing baby
who then began to weep.

Indigo watched the townsfolk
bar their gates and shut their doors.
He knew they did not want him
in their village, anymore.

"I have to go now, don't I?
I have to leave my home.
No one could stand beside me
while with a monster I must roam."

He started moving faster,
sure that he could not stay.
Yet when he turned a corner,
there were people in his way.

You see, what he'd forgotten,
or never understood,
was that he had a family
who loved him like they should.

His mother met him softly,
his father with a kiss,
and both, without a tremor, said,
"We will not run from this."

Around him, then, our boy saw
what he wondered to behold:
his friends were all together,
standing resolute and bold.

True, some had left him lonely,
but others took their place.
These new friends saw his dragon,
and they smiled in its face.

His mother took his hand then;
she wiped away a tear,
and leaning close against him,
she whispered in his ear:

"What you may be ashamed of,
what might seem strange and new,
what feels so black and hopeless,
is still a part of you."

"Dear one," said his father,
"you will never be alone.
Still, there are certain monsters
you must master on your own."

Our lad then saw quite clearly
the task that lay ahead,
so one last time he left them,
followed by the beast he led.

He walked past sneering neighbours,
faithless friends, and pompous foes.
He did not heed their slander,
nor their scorn did he oppose.

When he had come a distance
far away from all he passed,
he clamoured up a hillside
and halted there, at last.

With a breath, he lay his sword down;
though fear in him did rise,
he turned his head about and
looked his dragon in the eyes.

The creature did not waver,
did not snarl, did not blink.
It only seemed to listen
and to watch Indigo think.

"I'm through with this dark feeling,"
said the young boy, "I have cried.
I've hidden, fled, and fought you—
now it's time I learned to ride."

With eyes upon his dragon,
he waited for its bite.
But when it heard our hero's words,
it spread its wings for flight . . .

Within the little village,
eyes rose and jaws went slack
when Indigo came flying
upon his dragon's back.

At once, the townsfolk begged him
to tell them how he'd found
such power, grace, and beauty
to lift him from the ground.

"If you could only see," he said,
"what strength your strangeness brings!
Your monster may look fearsome, but
you'll find that it has wings."

His father helped him, beaming
as he gave his friends a ride.
His mother stood beside him,
and her face was touched with pride.

So Indigo was happy,
Indigo was free,
for he had no other secrets
that he feared for them to see.

Within, he'd found the courage
to transform the blackest night,
to gaze on what he dreaded
until shadows became light.

Now you may think this story
to be fable through and through,
but I'll wager you will find it,
in its essence, to be true.

The very beasts that haunt you
can also lift you high.
Don't ever fear your honest self—
be brave, climb up, and fly!

For those with dragons of their own (Krista)

Thank You!

The 10 Stories collection has been made possible through the generosity and love poured into these stories by our old friends and new, the writers and illustrators who all gave their wisdom and magic: Philip Ardagh, Avital Balwit, Jamie Beard, Sita Brahmachari, Eleanor Cullen, Danica Da Silva Pereira, Ria Dastidar, Alexis Deacon, Laura Dockrill, Jamila Gavin, Sahar Haghgoo, Jay Hulme, Daniel Ido, Krista M. Lambert, Jane Ray, Jacinta Read, Chris Riddell, David Roberts, Marcus Sedgwick, Anjali Tiwari. And through the kindness and devotion of the brilliant publishing editors, art directors and designers who volunteered their time to transform these great stories into even greater books: Emily Ball, Liz Bankes, Andrew Biscomb, Jane Buckley, Alice Curry, Holly Fulbrook, Lilly Gottwald, Elorine Grant, Libby Hamilton, Daisy Jellicoe, Txabi Jones, Ruth Knowles, Tiffany Leeson, Jacqui McDonough, Caroline Royds, Chloé Tartinville, Holly Tonks, Clare Whitston, Sean Williams. Huge gratitude to Matt Baxter and Lydia Fisher at Baxter & Bailey for donating their time to produce the 10 Stories brand, style and formats. If it wasn't for the 643 donors to our crowdfunding campaign, these books may never have made it to print - and we especially want to thank Rachel Denwood and Simon & Schuster, Sam Arthur and Nobrow, Michelle McLeod and Baillie Gifford, the CSR team at Linklaters LLP, Tim Bevan, Wolfgang Tillmans and all our former Board members for their generous support. Behind the scenes, the team and Board at Pop Up kept this great ship afloat through these most turbulent times, and we cannot thank them enough for always being part of the story no matter how hard the story gets.

Made possible by

 Baxter & Bailey